90 day approval
26-91
3.95

HEY, HAY!

A WAGONFUL OF
FUNNY HOMONYM RIDDLES

by Marvin Terban
illustrated by Kevin Hawkes

CLARION BOOKS • NEW YORK

To the memory of my father
Edward S. Terban
who loved the English language
because it meant freedom to him
M. T.

To my brother Chad
K.H.

Clarion Books
a Houghton Mifflin Company imprint
215 Park Avenue South, New York, NY 10003
Text copyright © 1991 by Marvin Terban
Illustrations copyright © 1991 by Kevin Hawkes
All rights reserved.
For information about permission to reproduce
selections from this book, write to Permissions,
Houghton Mifflin Company, 2 Park Street, Boston, MA 02108.
Printed in the USA

Library of Congress Cataloging-in-Publication Data

Terban, Marvin.
Hey, hay! : a wagonful of funny homonym riddles
by Marvin Terban ; illustrated by Kevin Hawkes
p.   cm.
Includes bibliographical references.
Summary: A collection of riddles based on homonyms, arranged
according to construction and level of difficulty.
ISBN 0-395-54431-9. — ISBN 0-395-56183-3 (pbk.)
1. Riddles, Juvenile. 2. English language—Homonyms—Juvenile
humor. [1. English language—Homonyms.
2. Riddles.] I.Hawkes, Kevin, ill. II. Title.
PN6371.5.T435 1991
818'.5402—dc20

BP 10 9 8 7 6 5 4 3 2 1

Contents

Introduction   5

1 · Sound-Alike Pairs   7

2 · Sentences With Sound-Alike Pairs   22

3 · Sound-Alike Triplets   37

4 · Triplet Sentences   41

5 · Four-Word Riddle Sentences   49

6 · HomoNames   53

Alphabetical List of the Homonyms
in This Book   61

Other Books About Homonyms/Homophones   64

Introduction

English is a confusing language with many tricky words. For instance, there are hundreds of words that sound exactly like hundreds of other words, but they are spelled differently and have different meanings. These sound-alike words can be called either homonyms or homophones.

Most homonyms/homophones come in pairs, as in the following sentence:

I **ate eight** apples.

Some come in triplets. For example:

Maize grows in **May's maze**.

There are even a few (very few, thank goodness!) quartets of homonyms/homophones. And people's names sometimes sound like other words. You'll find a special section of "HomoNames" in this book.

The challenging riddles and funny pictures that follow will help you identify and understand eighty-four sets of humorously hazardous homonyms/homophones. You'll find answers at the end of each chapter to help you unravel the ridiculous riddles. So, these **days** if you're in a **daze** about confusing words that sound alike but are spelled differently, take a ~~**peak**~~ ~~**pique**~~ **peek** at this book.

Sound-Alike Pairs

Here comes the first load in the wagonful of homonym riddles. The answer to each of the riddles in this chapter is a pair of sound-alike (but not spelled-alike) words.

   To get these homonyms hopping, here is a sample riddle. The answer is upside down at the bottom of this page.

Example: What do you call the person who inherits what we breathe?

   Now, here are more than two dozen riddles to challenge your homonymous skills. Remember, each answer is just two words that sound exactly alike. You'll find the answers at the end of this chapter on page 21. A helpful hint: The answers are all in alphabetical order from B to W. Good luck!

Answer: The **air heir.**

1. Mr. Scared was afraid to roll the ball down the alley to knock over the pins, but Mr. . . .

2. The person who rents a room on the boundary between countries is a . . . ?

3. What do you call a hiding place for money?

4. Who wants you to buy a basement?

5. When Mr. Cornseed became an army officer, what was he called?

6. What do you do when you abandon the sweets at the
   end of a meal?

7.   What happens when female deer take a nap?

8.   What is soft, thick hair on a pinelike evergreen tree?

9.   How did our honored visitor find out the secret?

10. If a large, powerful African ape joins a band of fighters that hide in trees, ambush the enemy, and go on sudden raids, what do you call him?

11. Healthy pieces of ice that fall from the sky are . . . ?

12. What do you shout to get the attention of cut and dried grass?

13.   This year's fashionable country hotel is the . . .

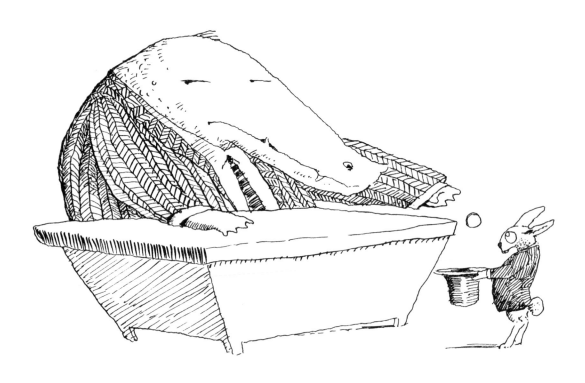

14.   What did the banker call the only sum of money he lent
      to a borrower?

15. What fastening devices do you use to protect your smoked salmon?

16. What award do you win for sticking your nose into other people's business?

17. What do we call sixty minutes that belong to us alone?

18. What does a traveling salesman do with the parts of a bicycle that you push with your feet?

19. What is the money a fortune-teller makes from his business?

20. A genuine, authentic spool for film is a . . .

21. When a store sells canvas that catches wind on a boat at bargain prices, it's called a . . .

22. How do you say, "Get away, footwear!"

23. What is writing paper that does not move?

24. What is money that the government collects on the sale of little nails?

25. What did the land frog do when his car broke down?

26. Seven days that are not strong are a . . .

Answers to Sound-Alike Pairs

1. **Bold bowled.**
2. **Border boarder.**
3. A **cash cache**.
4. A **cellar seller**.
5. **Colonel Kernel.**
6. **Desert dessert**.
7. **Does doze**.
8. **Fir fur**.
9. Our **guest guessed**.
10. A **guerrilla gorilla**.
11. **Hale hail**.
12. **"Hey, hay!"**
13. **In inn**.
14. The **lone loan**.
15. **Lox locks**.
16. The **meddle medal**.
17. **Our hour**.
18. **Peddles pedals**.
19. **Prophet profit**.
20. **Real reel**.
21. **Sail sale**.
22. **"Shoo, shoe!"**
23. **Stationary stationery**.
24. **Tacks tax**.
25. **Toad towed**.
26. **Weak week**.

·2·

Sentences With
Sound-Alike Pairs

To solve these puzzles, try to say each of the following sentences in a different way. Think of homonym pairs to substitute for the words in dark print.

Example: In this library, you are **permitted** to talk **in a voice that can be heard**.
Answer: In this library, you are **allowed** to talk **aloud**.

Here are twenty-five more homonym riddle sentences. The full answer sentences are given at the end of this chapter on page 35. Hint: The first words of all the answers in this chapter are in alphabetical order from A to W.

27. Walter, don't **change** the **table where the religious ceremonies are performed**.

28. When he saw that he was **hairless**, he **sobbed loudly**.

29. The carpenter **charged** me for what he was going to **construct**.

30. I **select** the same gum he **grinds with his teeth**.

31. Hit the **circular metal plate** whenever the **representation** of liberty is shown.

Shoe Colors
Black
White
Tan
Cordovan

32. She'll **stop living** if they **color** her shoes the wrong shade.

33. When he couldn't **locate** the missing jewels, he was **made to pay** $1000.00 by the judge.

34.   When she saw how much it had **increased in size**, she started to **make deep sounds of grief**.

35. Those **fellows** betrayed us under the **false appearance** of friendship.

36. They **give jobs** to workers on a **more elevated** floor.

37. I sang a **religious song** with **that man**.

38. He is very **negligent** because he **does not have** discipline.

39. She **rented** the car that cost the **smallest amount of** money.

40. He's a **fib teller** if he says he knows how to play that
ancient Greek harp.

41. Would you **object** if I **dug** for gold here?

42. They signed the peace **treaty** in a **very crowded** room.

43. When the bells **ring out** loudly, **take the skins off** the bananas.

44. If you sign this **portion** of paper, you'll have **freedom from war**.

45. She took a **public opinion survey** while sitting on a **long, slender piece of wood**.

46. Does this **line of stitching** really **appear** to be crooked?

47. After he **put new bottoms on** the shoes, he **took money for** them.

48. He showed a lot of **skill in handling difficult situations** when he **nailed** up his apology.

49. The sailor **instructed** us to keep the rope **tightly drawn**.

50. The boat was **fastened with a rope** so that it wouldn't float away with the **rise and fall of the ocean**.

51. You must be **put onto a scale** before you may **walk into the water**.

Answers to Sentences
with Sound-Alike Pairs

27. Walter, don't **alter** the **altar**.
28. When he saw that he was **bald**, he **bawled**.
29. The carpenter **billed** me for what he was going to **build**.
30. I **choose** the same gum he **chews**.
31. Hit the **cymbal** whenever the **symbol** of liberty is shown.
32. She'll **die** if they **dye** her shoes the wrong shade.
33. When he couldn't **find** the missing jewels, he was **fined** $1000.00 by the judge.
34. When she saw how much it had **grown**, she started to **groan**.
35. Those **guys** betrayed us under the **guise** of friendship.
36. They **hire** workers on a **higher** floor.
37. I sang a **hymn** with **him**.
38. He is very **lax** because he **lacks** discipline.
39. She **leased** the car that cost the **least** money.
40. He's a **liar** if he says he knows how to play that **lyre**.
41. Would you **mind** if I **mined** for gold here?
42. They signed the peace **pact** in a **packed** room.
43. When the bells **peal** loudly, **peel** the bananas.
44. If you sign this **piece** of paper, you'll have **peace**.
45. She took a **poll** while sitting on a **pole**.
46. Does this **seam** really **seem** to be crooked?
47. After he **soled** the shoes, he **sold** them.

48. He showed a lot of **tact** when he **tacked** up his apology.
49. The sailor **taught** us to keep the rope **taut**.
50. The boat was **tied** so it wouldn't float away with the **tide**.
51. You must be **weighed** before you may **wade**.

⚬**3**⚬

Sound-Alike Triplets

As if sound-alike pairs weren't tricky enough, sometimes homonyms come in triplets. Here are five riddles with three-word answers. All three words are spelled differently but sound exactly the same.

Example: What do you call the conceited wind-direction indicator blood vessel?
Answer: **Vain vane vein.**

The answers to the triplet riddles are printed at the end of this chapter on page 40. For an extra challenge, the answers are not in alphabetical order. No helpful hints this time. You're on your own!

52. What do you call the most important neck hair on a horse in a New England state?

53. What words describe a person whose clothing is totally filled with rips and tears but who is saintly?

54. What do you call a short, simple country poem about a lazy but greatly loved person?

55. How would you write a three-word headline that says, "The recently arrived, large South African antelope was aware of the facts"?

56. That lady also had twins. In other words, she gave birth . . .

Answers to Sound-Alike Triplets

52. **Main Maine mane**.
53. **Wholly holey holy**.
54. **Idle idol idyll**.
55. **"New Gnu Knew"**
56. **To two too**.

Triplet Sentences

Try to say each of these sentences a different way by changing the words in dark print into homonym/homophone triplets.

Example: **They are** over **in that place** in **the "owned-by-them"** house.
They're over **there** in **their** house.

The full answer sentences are at the end of this chapter on page 48. As an added challenge for you, the riddle sentences get longer and longer. And the answers are not in alphabetical order. Good luck!

57. **Farewell**! I'm going **via** bus to **purchase** some things.

58. While I **traveled** down the **highway**, she **paddled** up the river.

59. Stand by the **evergreen tree** in the dew, **thou** new **female sheep**.

60. When I **see** the right **place**, I will **quote a passage from** Shakespeare.

61. **I will** walk down the **passage between the rows of seats** on the **small island**.

62. When the pirate **observes** ships on the **oceans**, he tries to **capture** them.

63. When I **lift** my hand, **demolish** that building so we'll get more of the sun's **beams**.

64. In which **subdivision of the city** did the **small donkey** try to **dig a hole in the ground**?

65. The accountant **totals** the cost of **advertisements** for this **axlike timber-trimming tool**.

66. I was in a fit of **resentment** when he climbed the **mountaintop** to take a **secret look** at what I was doing.

67. I caught a **contagious viral disease with fever and muscle pain** when a cold wind **moved through the air** down the **chimney pipe**.

68. The **dish made of chopped meat, red peppers, and kidney beans** from **a country on the Pacific coast of South America** is **fairly cold**.

Answers to Triplet Sentences

57. **'Bye**! I'm going **by** bus to **buy** some things.
58. While I **rode** down the **road**, she **rowed** up the river.
59. Stand by the **yew** in the dew, **you** new **ewe**.
60. When I **sight** the right **site**, I will **cite** Shakespeare.
61. **I'll** walk down the **aisle** on the **isle**.
62. When the pirate **sees** ships on the **seas**, he tries to **seize** them.
63. When I **raise** my hand, **raze** that building so we'll get more of the sun's **rays**.
64. In which **borough** did the **burro** try to **burrow**?
65. The accountant **adds** the cost of **ads** for this **adz**.
66. I was in a fit of **pique** when he climbed the **peak** to take a **peek** at what I was doing.
67. I caught a **flu** when a cold wind **flew** down the **flue**.
68. The **chili** from **Chile** is **chilly**.

Four-Word Riddle
Sentences

There are very few homonym quartets—groups of four words that sound exactly alike but are spelled differently. Here are four examples, but each one contains a word that is either poetic or obsolete (no longer used). You might not be able to figure them all out, but you still might have fun trying to guess at least three of the four words in each homonym quartet. Sentences with blank lines will show you where the missing words fit in. The full answer sentences are on page 52.

Now go **forward** to solve these **four-word** riddles!

69. It's good judgment to spend a few pennies for pleasant odors to perfume the room with the vapor of burning fragrances.

It's good _____ to spend a few _____ for _____ to _____ the room.

70. Hey, you! Hello, tall man. Hasten home.

_____ ! _____ , _____ man. _____ home.

71. To get the rock that bears minerals, you can swim; your other choice is to use a paddle to row over the lake.

To get the _____ , you can either swim _____ use an _____ to row _____ the lake.

72. Put down words about the formal ceremony correctly,
    person who creates plays.

    _____ about the _____ _____ , play _____ .

Answers to Four-Word
Riddle Sentences

69. It's good **sense** to spend a few **cents** for pleasant **scents** to **cense** the room.
70. **Heigh! Hi, high** man. **Hie** home.
71. To get the **ore**, you can either swim **or** use an **oar** to row **o'er** the lake.
72. **Write** about the **rite right**, play**wright**.

HomoNames

People's names can sometimes sound like other words.

In each of the following sentences, a name belongs on the blank line. Each sentence contains at least one clue to the missing name. The clues are words that sound exactly like the names that belong on the blank lines. But the clues are spelled differently from the names.

See if you can spot the clue words in the sentences and then figure out the names that belong on the blank lines. The answers are at the end of the chapter on page 60.

73.   Please fill up the tank, _____ .

74. Who dug up the treasure, _____ ?

75. Here is your costume for the Sioux tribal dance, _____ .

76. It would be better to lift weights at the gym, _____ .

77. Please load this peat moss into the wagon, _____ .

78. They'll raise a hue and cry if you hew down this tree, _____ .

79. You can be the bee in the class bug play, _____ .

80. Can you see more with your new telescope, _____ ?

81. He fell into the well when he heard the knell of the bell,
_____ .

82. Please help me carry this box, _____ .

83. Kneel down and see if it rolled under the bed, _____ .

84. I order you to seize 'er, _____ !

Answers to HomoNames

73. Please **fill** up the tank, **Phil**.
74. Who **dug** up the treasure, **Doug**?
75. Here is your costume for the **Sioux** tribal dance, **Sue**.
76. It would be better to lift weights at the **gym**, **Jim**.
77. Please load this **peat** moss into the wagon, **Pete**.
78. They'll raise a **hue** and cry if you **hew** down this tree, **Hugh**.
79. You can **be** the **bee** in the class bug play, **Bea**.
80. Can you **see more** with your new telescope, **Seymour**?
81. He fell into the well when he heard the **knell** of the bell, **Nell**.
82. Please help me **carry** this box, **Carrie**.
83. **Kneel** down and see if it rolled under the bed, **Neal**.
84. I order you to **seize 'er**, **Caesar**!

Alphabetical List of
the Homonyms in This Book

Homonym	Page	Homonym	Page	Homonym	Page
adds	48	buy	48	does	21
ads	48	by	48	Doug	60
adz	48	bye	48	doze	21
air	7	cache	21	dug	60
aisle	48	Caesar	60	dye	35
allowed	22	Carrie	60	eight	5
aloud	22	carry	60	ewe	48
altar	35	cash	21	fill	60
alter	35	cellar	21	find	35
ate	5	cense	52	fined	35
bald	35	cents	52	fir	21
bawled	35	chews	35	flew	48
be	60	Chile	48	flu	48
Bea	60	chili	48	flue	48
bee	60	chilly	48	forward	49
billed	35	choose	35	four-word	49
boarder	21	cite	48	fur	21
bold	21	colonel	21	gnu	40
border	21	cymbal	35	gorilla	21
borough	48	days	5	groan	35
bowled	21	daze	5	grown	35
build	35	desert	21	guerrilla	21
burro	48	dessert	21	guessed	21
burrow	48	die	35	guest	21

Homonym	Page	Homonym	Page	Homonym	Page
guise	35	Jim	60	o'er	52
guys	35	kernel	21	or	52
gym	60	kneel	60	ore	52
hail	21	knell	60	our	21
hale	21	knew	40	packed	35
hay	21	lacks	35	pact	35
heigh	52	lax	35	peace	35
heir	7	leased	35	peak	5, 48
hew	60	least	35	peal	35
hey	21	liar	35	peat	60
hi	52	loan	21	pedals	21
hie	52	locks	21	peddles	21
high	52	lone	21	peek	5, 48
higher	35	lox	21	peel	35
him	35	lyre	35	Pete	60
hire	35	main	40	Phil	60
holey	40	Maine	40	piece	35
holy	40	maize	5	pique	5, 48
hour	21	mane	40	pole	35
hue	60	May's	5	poll	35
Hugh	60	maze	5	profit	21
hymn	35	medal	21	prophet	21
idle	40	meddle	21	raise	48
idol	40	mind	35	rays	48
idyll	40	mined	35	raze	48
I'll	48	Neal	60	real	21
in	21	Nell	60	reel	21
inn	21	new	40	right	52
isle	48	oar	52	rite	52

Homonym	Page	Homonym	Page	Homonym	Page
road	48	Sioux	60	to	40
rode	48	site	48	toad	21
rowed	48	sold	35	too	40
sail	21	soled	35	towed	21
sale	21	stationary	21	two	40
scents	52	stationery	21	vain	37
seam	35	Sue	60	vane	37
seas	48	symbol	35	vein	37
seem	35	tacked	36	wade	36
see more	60	tacks	21	weak	21
sees	48	tact	36	week	21
seize	48	taught	36	weighed	36
seize 'er	60	taut	36	wholly	40
seller	21	tax	21	-wright	52
sense	52	their	41	write	52
Seymour	60	there	41	yew	48
shoe	21	they're	41	you	48
shoo	21	tide	36		
sight	48	tied	36		

Other Books About
Homonyms/Homophones

If you're interested in learning more about sound-alike words, you might like to read some of the following books the author used in his research.

The American Heritage Dictionary of the English Language, Boston: Houghton Mifflin, 1981.

Franklyn, Julian. **Which Witch?** New York: Dorset Press, 1987

Harrison, James S. **Confusion Reigns**. New York: St. Martin's Press, 1987.

Heacock, Paul. **Which Word When?** New York: A Laurel Book, Dell Publishing, 1989.

Kilpatrick, James J. **The Ear Is Human**. Kansas City: Andrews, McMeel & Parker, 1985.

Maestro, Giulio. **What's Mite Might? Homophone Riddles to Boost Your Word Power**! New York: Clarion Books, 1986.

Scholastic Dictionary of Synonyms, Antonyms, Homonyms. New York: Scholastic, Inc., 1965.

Terban, Marvin. **Eight Ate: A Feast of Homonym Riddles**. New York: Clarion Books, 1982.